W
VISITING
BABETTE

KAT MEADS

© 2025 by Kat Meads

All Rights Reserved.

Set in Mrs Eaves XL with LaTeX.

ISBN: 978-1-963846-24-9 (paperback)
ISBN: 978-1-963846-25-6 (ebook)
Library of Congress Control Number: 2024946158

Sagging Meniscus Press
Montclair, New Jersey
saggingmeniscus.com

*[That song about fairy tales coming true
and happening to you]*

WHILE VISITING BABETTE

[A beginning consisting of sharp turns and sharper surprise]

ONE

Ina had visited Babette in a variety of structures, ranging from a gabled Victorian in the woods to a sprawling ranch on a hilltop with a distant view of the sea. The most memorable was a sleek fabrication of severe right angles, very modern but somehow also very hot. There, Babette had stripped off her clothes, prompting the medicos to add "exhibitionism" to her chart when really Babette was just hot. The clothes Babette had been forced to put back on trapped both heat and sweat and Babette had developed a nasty rash. After Babette was transferred, the rash subsided. A faint rash ring remained near Babette's elbow, but it too was fading. By and large Babette's skin had called off its revolt.

Running late, Ina ran up the stone steps of the facility and continued to jog through strangely empty hallways. She usually had to check in and confirm her family connection before proceeding, but since no one sat behind the registration desk and she knew the location of Babette's third floor quarters, she jogged on, knocked faintly as a courtesy to her cousin and entered.

Babette lay on the bed, looking like a languid saint, gaze canted toward a corner of the ceiling, a pose she maintained.

Ina took no offense. Babette never immediately acknowledged her presence. Strangers appeared in Babette's domain at every hour of the day and night, peering, querying. There was no reason for Babette to assume the person in the room was a relative who had genuinely come to visit.

Because Ina did not want to rush Babette's process by crowding the bed, she took a seat on the floor, back against the wall. Ina might have preferred sitting on the floor even if there had been a chair. The floor was spotlessly clean. Once upon a time in-room chairs had been provided for visitors, but a resident—not Babette—had tried to use one as a battering ram to break the window and thereafter chair privileges had been revoked.

At the time Babette mused: "I wonder how, after breaking glass, she planned to get past the bars."

"It's a question," Ina had said because that was what she thought, and for a while Ina and Babette jointly pondered the unanswerable together.

Waiting today for Babette to intuit their cousinship, knees cocked, Ina noticed scuffs on her shoes. The pristine floor had thrown their scuffiness into relief. Ina was tempted—but only tempted—to lick a finger and swipe at the leather when such a touch-up was indefinitely deferred by a tremendous crash on the floor above, followed by what sounded like a stampede.

Babette turned her way.

"Hello, cousin," she said and smiled.

On her butt Ina scooted over to Babette's bedside.

"Apologies for the noise," Babette said.

"What noise?" Ina asked.

After which they both teehee-ed as they had when, as children, they lied in unison.

Today, by Babette's instigation, they discussed blue, a broad topic quickly narrowed to a blue jar belonging to their Aunt Careen.

Above the noise above their heads, they spoke in blue jar terms.

—Oval.

—More round, than oval.

—A chip in the lid.

—Two chips.

—Rose petals inside.

—Licorice.

—Marbles.

—Seashells.

It was not a contentious discussion, nothing close to an argument. Both Ina and Babette were fully aware that people rarely agreed on what had occurred the moment before, much less on the details of childhood. They carried on their remembering with no investment in achieving a memory merge or in persuading the other of the superiority of her recollection. Such intention would have been ludicrous.

Because Ina was still sitting on the floor and also because she and Babette were deep in the wallows of reminiscing, Ina had ceased to pay close attention to the noise that had left the fourth floor, taken the stairs, and spilled onto Babette's hallway with an added component: jangling keys. The result was that Ina had not with the necessary speed scrambled to her feet, gained the door, identified herself to whomever stood on the other side and clarified the cause of her visitor card-less state before a key engaged the lock on Babette's door.

Ina and Babette had not finished visiting. Until prevented, Ina had been in no hurry to leave.

Appalled in advance at the stupid predictability of her reactions, Ina embarked on a standard course of useless countermeasures: wrenching the doorknob, pounding on the door itself, shouting for help, demanding some unknown someone come immediately to her rescue.

Embarrassing behavior, start to finish.

ONE

"You could hide under my bed," Babette offered, not quite as spot on as Babette typically was in reading Ina's thoughts. In any case Babette's single bed had no bed skirt and was not much of a hiding place, clean though the floor beneath appeared to be.

Regardless, it was kind of Babette to offer.

"If worse comes to worst," Ina said.

Babette nodded.

The commotion now seemed to be centered farther away, somewhere in the vicinity of the front lawn.

Ina remained seated on the floor. Babette, supine, resumed staring at a corner of the ceiling. Despite the room being almost chilly, Ina realized she was sweating. Babette sneezed once, a jolting, violent sneeze, then returned to a state of tranquility. Ina dabbed at her sweaty armpits. Judging by the slant of the light, it was late afternoon before the footsteps of another someone with keys approached Babette's door.

Correctly reading Ina's thoughts on this occasion, Babette swiftly summarized the problem. Even if Ina got through the door and made a dash for the parking lot she would, due to current circumstances, be taken for an escapee, grabbed, hustled back inside and very likely deposited in a room other than Babette's where Ina would enjoy no company at all.

And yet the moment the door budged, Ina could not help herself. She rushed forward, shoving hard at the obstacle between herself and the hallway, a sequence with consequences preordained.

"I told you to hide, cousin," Babette said sorrowfully though not in reprimand, which Ina greatly appreciated.

Notwithstanding Babette's exquisite tact, they each knew what they knew.

A rookie, Ina had made a rookie mistake.

[A middle that will not continue forever despite what the propagandists imply]

TWO

BABETTE CAME TO SEE INA very early the next morning.

"Oh good," Babette said. "You did get a room to yourself after all."

Ina glanced about. It was a room but it did not feel like a room that was ownable. Certainly not by her. Despite the stunning cleanliness of the whole, Ina had noticed a thin strand of brown hair curled like a snail in the corner. She could not bring herself to disturb it.

Babette became distracted.

"Someone must have moved on for a room to be vacant."

If Ina's thoughts had been less in disarray, she would have interrogated Babette at once. The term "moved on" contained too many possibilities.

From Ina's window, Babette's search of the grounds was of limited scope. Part of Ina wanted to join Babette at the window but another part refused to allow it. Since yesterday Ina's complicated feelings about windows had become more complicated.

"Babette?"

"Ina?"

"Babette?"

"Ina?"

Round robin callouts had been one of their childhood routines. Babette was teasing but still kept her back turned to Ina, scanning the visible grounds.

The situation all around was really quite a mess.

When Babette joined her on the bed, Ina noticed a tiny vein pulsing in Babette's wrist. Babette's next words did not sound as composed as Babette's comments generally sounded.

"Don't worry. You'll be allowed to leave the room tomorrow."

Ina nodded, although leaving the room was not what she had been thinking about and once again Babette had misread her thoughts. Babette not being able to read her thoughts made Ina feel lonelier than a willow seed.

"Who moved on, do you think?" Ina asked because the determination seemed to mean so much to Babette.

"It could have been anyone," Babette said.

It was an answer not in the least like Babette's usual answers. Babette was a great believer in the existence of solid answers, hard as they might be to find. When they were children, Ina could never muse in a conversational way: "How far do you think Aunt Careen's porch is from the car?" or the like without Babette setting off for a tape measure.

"You'll figure it out," Ina said for Babette's sake.

Although even if Babette discovered who was missing and told Ina, Ina would be none the wiser. Ina only knew one person here. Babette. She could not be introduced to the gone. But she would, as the days went by, be introduced to the others still here. Then, if another someone moved on, like Babette she would be scanning in vain for a hat or raincoat or outstretched arm on the grounds below.

A tremendous grumpiness overtook and displaced Ina's gloom.

"Stop," Babette said. "Grinding your teeth won't help."

Ina did not argue but she did sulk.

What a foolish, foolish girl she had been yesterday.

THREE

INA AND BABETTE seemed to have the side yard to themselves. The bench they sat on tilted downhill. Both used their feet as body brakes. Neither wished to tumble. The weather had reversed itself since morning. The sky had emptied itself of scudding clouds. No wind whipped anything anywhere.

Ina gazed upon the hedge of azaleas with blossoms pink as gums. The blooms pressed together in solidarity but their pinkness made blending a non-starter. As a child more than once and without remorse, Ina had shot at azalea blossoms to perfect her slingshot aim. She must have been a thoroughly caddish child, Ina thought.

Thinking the worst of herself was very discouraging.

Babette snatched up Ina's hand, raised it above Ina's head and flapped it to flap away gloomy thoughts.

Babette was not one to dwell on past errors.

The afternoon was warming up nicely. Scores of bugs crawled along the bench arms and uneven ground. In the distance a groundskeeper started up a lawnmower. It was now the season of striving grass. Coming toward them was someone in a loose shift with dangling waist ties. She wasn't wearing any shoes at all, not even her outside slippers.

"Hello," she said.

"Hello," Ina said.

"Hello, Clara," Babette said.

At the sound of her name, Clara blushed. The smile that split Clara's face improved her overall appearance by quite a lot, Ina thought.

"I've come to read you a story," Clara said.

"How lovely," Babette said.

Ina shifted uneasily on the bench, one of an audience of two who could be plainly seen by the performer. She would have to make sure not to frown.

Clara raised pages of paper to her chest and jutted her elbows. A mosquito landed on Ina's arm but she dared not interrupt Clara's preparations by slapping it dead. When Ina and Babette were young and the nights hot at Aunt Careen's, they often sat in front of the screen door on the off-chance car lights would pass and illuminate the mosquito squad trying frantically to get through the mesh. Mosquito desperation sounded like a song.

Babette had gone very still, waiting for Clara to begin. The mosquito bore in.

"It's called 'Sister Stuff,'" Clara said. "I wrote it for you."

Not a bad title, Ina thought. Babette nodded.

"I wrote it *about* you two," Clara emphasized.

Again Babette nodded but Ina could not prevent the maturing of a frown. She did not like the idea of being written about.

In preparation Clara briefly raised her heels and stood on tiptoe, then flat-footed began to read.

The Sisters Belvedere are not of our time. They sprang forth from the early trenches of the previous century and came of age during the Flapper era when women, freed from the corset, were presumed to have all a female heart could desire. Louise, the elder, is out and about; Sophie has not yet parted from the sheets but has begun to stretch her arms to the ceiling and yawn, in no hurry to discover what the day might bring.

Clara did not write this, Ina thought.

"Or did she?" Babette said aloud.

Clara continued.

In short order the day brings:

From Louise's fiancé, his foot crushed in the door of the sisters' hotel room: "Louise! Louise! I can explain!"

From Louise: "Never!"

THREE

After stomping on the protruding foot until it retreats, Louise kicks the door completely shut, locks it and begins to massacre the bundle of tweedia, feverfew, hellebore, ranunculus, stephanotis, allium, cosmos, lysimachia, baby's breath, snapdragon, sweet pea, fern and whatnot she holds in hand, first by savagely beating the engagement bouquet against the door and then, as she circles the room, against every wall until every bloom is demolished and every stalk decapitated. This mission takes quite some time, time Sophie spends in a state of anxious alarm, sheets gathered to her neck. Sophie is wise to worry. Once Louise finishes attacking the walls, she turns on her sister. Advancing, she glares.

"I can explain!" Sophie yelps before being pelted with flower stalks. "He said I had lovely feet. You know how I've always been self-conscious about my feet."

Ina was growing perturbed. She and Babette were nothing like Louise and Sophie. They were cousins, not sisters. Neither had ever been engaged. Neither had shame-inducing feet.

Having tired out her arms, mussed her bob and twisted her low of neck/short of hem Flapper dress, Louise flings aside her weapon, flops onto the un-slept-in bed beside her sister's, removes her shoes and begins, pointedly, to rub her exquisitely lovely feet.

"And?"

"And?"

"He complimented your disgusting feet, and . . .?"

"And I'm *sorry*, Louise. Really, really I am."

The mosquito bite was itching ferociously. Ina was having trouble concentrating. But if Sophie was the apologizer, she must be Sophie. Babette did not hold her slip-ups against herself.

The apology is lubricated by very convincing tears from Sophie, who tries never to cry because, as she's been told on numerous occasions by both men and women, she is an unattractive crier who should avoid crying in company—even her family's company—at all costs. What is not often said about Sophie and her crying is that her tears dry remarkably fast.

It was true. Ina did look a mess when weeping. She manufactured very large tears that did not so much stream as bounce down her cheeks. If Ina failed to wipe her face, some of the tear water rebounded onto her clothes, completely skipping her neck.

"But . . . Louise?"

Having made her comparative foot point, Louise leaves off fondling her arches and focuses on fixing her disordered hair.

"Be honest. You don't care that much about him."

"Says who?"

"A lot of people."

"A lot of people who?"

"Well, Mama, for one."

At the M word, Louise's glare reanimates.

Although Babette had not stirred, Ina felt a vibration pass between them. They had no mothers, only aunts. As such they were perhaps not the best audience for mother mocking stories.

"Mama thinks you were, you know, bored as usual when he asked to marry you and bored you decided: *why not*."

Her sister *is* listening, Sophie can tell, because a listening Louise always licks her lips. Rarely, if ever, listened to, an emboldened Sophie elaborates.

"And, Louise? You know what else I think? I think I actually did you a favor. Because a fellow who'll sleep with his fiancée's sister will sleep with just about anyone."

The story's conclusion was fast approaching. Clara held up the final page whose backside preserved a food stain in the shape of an antelope.

In less time than it took to destroy her ex-fiancé's engagement bouquet, Louise considers her sister's argument. Before the rehearsal dinner, she and Sophie had planned to tour the fabulous city and eat a fabulous lunch on their own, sans men or mother. They could still do that—certainly they could—despite the other nonsense. Eventually Louise reaches for the map on the nightstand between them, unfolding it in squares. Its legend promises circles, arcs, parks, spires, towers, grottos, fountains, rivers with bridges, gardens with benches, statues with dragons, monuments with harps, celebrations of battle, commemorations of beheadings and whatnot.

On the map, the city does not look boring.

Clara curtsied. Babette clapped. Ina imitated Babette. Ina hoped they would not be quizzed on content. One of her mosquito bites had turned fiery red and another was percolating.

"Thank you, Clara," Babette said. "Ina and I will try, like the Sisters Belvedere, to avoid boredom at all costs."

Ina looked at Babette, who could be quite sharp in her joking. But Babette gave no appearance of joking.

Clara blushed, curtsied again and ran off with her pages.

"We are not much like Sophie and Louise," Ina said, hoping for confirmation.

"We are female," Babette said as if that settled the matter.

The sunlight was fading, as it will. The lawnmower had cut out. Nonspecific curses wafted over the landscape.

"I suppose I should have clapped harder," Ina said.

"You'll have another chance."

"Say more, please."

"Clara reads a story to any two sitting on a bench."

As shocked as Ina felt by Babette's revelation, the depth of her disappointment shocked her more. Ina had doubted the story was about her and Babette but then she had accepted the idea, trusted it, and now felt bereft.

She and Babette had not had a story written about them after all.

They just lived.

FOUR

INA'S ROOM was a replica of Babette's with one exception. Babette preferred to rest and sleep in the middle of a room, all walls at a distance. Before Ina had attempted to break out and they were locked in together, she and Babette, working as a team, had slid Babette's bed to the middle of the room.

Having her bed in the middle of the room turned Babette almost giddy. After the incident, Babette kept the bed where it was but the giddiness, as giddiness tends to do, faded.

Ina's bed was also iron, also white, also single. She and Babette had debated which of their beds sported more layers of paint. As Ina soon learned, it was important not to absentmindedly pick at her bedframe because picked-at paint flaked off, accumulated and marred an otherwise spotless floor.

Paint chips on a floor pleased no one.

However, as Babette pointed out, an enterprising someone might make a project of arranging the paint chips in a way that passed for outsider art. It was an interesting notion but beyond Ina's talents. Her pushed around paint chips resembled spiky mudpies, nothing grander.

Ina had given the position of her own bed considerable thought as, following the incident, she had given all doors, whether locked or unlocked, considerable thought. She could not have abided having her bed in the middle of the room like Babette, a position she did not for a second doubt would generate a run of unmoored raft and floating banshee dreams.

"Did you crack your window last night?" Babette invariably inquired at the beginning of their morning visits because both Babette and Aunt Careen were staunch believers in the benefits of night ventilation and because Aunt Careen used the term cracked window to mean a window opened a smidge and neither Ina nor Babette had ever been able to improve on the description and declined to truck with an inferior one.

No one objected to anyone cracking the window to let in a little night air, Babette assured Ina.

But even if Ina did steel herself to touch and crack her window, she did not want to sleep *under* a window. First, because she was unwilling to provide no-see-ums with a quicker meal. Second, because windows frequently dripped at night. The closer someone was to a drip, the louder the drip sounded. That assessment was irrefutable.

Ina was also not a fan of beds jammed flush against walls, which made the wall side of the bed impossible to make up in a non-lopsided way. Another strike against the bed-against-wall configuration was its invitation to injury. Once a long while ago, Ina had gotten so worked up in and by a nightmare that she had flung out her arms to stop the dream car she rode in from hurtling downhill and clunked her right elbow so hard against the wall that she had given herself a painful blueberry-blue bruise that took weeks to dissolve.

The most practical solution to the dilemma—which Ina had discussed at length with Babette—seemed to be to cattycorner the headboard, leaving plenty of flinging space on either side of the mattress.

Babette approved.

Ina had been awake and dressed since dawn because, truthfully, she had not yet adjusted to sleeping in a cattycornered bed, which meant she was more alert than a deep sleeper would have been to the early morning racket filtering through the cracked window. Birds chirped with spirit. The lawn sprinklers hissed and sputtered. In the distance thunder rolled. Nearer and less faintly somebody squealed.

FOUR

The squeal did not sound altogether joyous. If it had sounded joyous, Ina almost certainly would have stuck with her policy of steering clear of windows.

Because Ina's room was, like Babette's, on the third floor, the pond was easily visible. Ina would not have needed to resort to binoculars to spy on the pond even if she had binoculars at the ready. Ina recognized Isabelle because she recognized Isabelle's hair braid, long as a black snake. The others were shadowed by trees. The splashing about had temporarily disturbed the green algae and sent it cowering to the sides of the pond, but as soon as the fun and games were done the algae would recover its territory. Algae always did.

There were no shoes on the grass. All must have run into the pond without bothering to take off their shoes.

Ina counted heads as one might count the heads of otters poking out of a bay. Five beings with water-plastered hair wore water-soaked shifts that clung to their ribs as they leapt up and sideways.

A mob of four was pushing under a fifth.

"Stop that!" Ina shouted, trying with volume and bluster to sound like the Lord of the Pond.

Four heads pivoted in her direction. The fifth surfaced, coughing.

It was the sputterer, the former squealer, who first yelled at Ina to bugger off. In no time at all, the others took up the chant. Reunited, all five squealed.

Ina left the window and returned to bed, unmaking it to get in again. Her heart was thumping wildly. She pulled the sheets and blankets to her chin. The sheets smelled of strong soap. The blanket smelled of moth balls. She wished Babette had been standing alongside her at the window. Babette would have known whether anyone had been truly in danger. Babette could always gauge. Ina was the one who misinterpreted.

FIVE

To cheer up Ina, Babette proposed the quotes game. Each would scour the library's four shelves of books and select five favorite sentences.

"Five, or . . . ?"

"Or ten or twenty or fifty-three," Babette said.

Aunt Careen had invented the game after Ina and Babette had moved into Aunt Careen's house for keeps. It had been a long, long while since Ina had played. Perhaps Babette had played the game with someone else before Ina had come to visit and stayed.

"I'm not sure I'll . . ." Ina said.

"You'll remember," Babette said.

Assured by Babette's assurances Ina relaxed and as a relaxed person did feel more cheerful.

To keep their selections secret until the game officially started, Ina and Babette agreed not to share the single library table and swore on their honor not to invent an excuse to pass by the other and let their eyes wander.

The library was a forgotten place. There was grit on the floor. Waiting for Babette to finish her turn, Ina counted cobwebs.

Babette whizzed past the four shelves, plucking books as if they were dandelions. It was the fastest Ina had seen Babette move in ages but the speed did not render Babette dizzy. In more leisurely fashion, Babette set up camp on the library couch. The library couch had also been forgotten except by the mice. There were mice nests inside the chewed green cushions. Apart from the mice, there were droplets of blood here and there on the couch arms. An odor somewhat like sweat but danker escaped from the couch the moment it was called upon to support a girl, thin or fat.

Her turn, Ina studied the four shelves of books from afar. If the shelves of books were a map, the map would have been mostly brown and gray with occasional patches of faded red and blue. Hard as those faded reds and blues worked to entrance her, Ina worked to resist. She had been fooled by showiness before.

Having settled on her choices from across the room, Ina darted forward for the snatch.

On the couch, Babette had already unfurled her paper. Each had been allowed a sheet of foolscap and stick of charcoal. When they left the library, the charcoal had to stay behind but the paper could travel. At the end of the hour, Ina folded her page many times over. Babette rolled hers into a cylinder and used it as a spyglass as they walked the hallway.

On reveal day they sat cross-legged on the floor of Babette's room. The gleaming linoleum had just been waxed.

Babette gave the signal and both started shouting at once.

" 'The waves are louder when it's dark out.' "

" 'Mr. Marshall was dressed in the dreadful neatness which distinguishes the male relatives of accused persons.' "

" 'No imagination! That's what makes a beast.' "

" 'As every homemaker knows, the less furniture there is the easier it is to clean.' "

" 'She was more highly placed than I in the hierarchy of individual charm.' "

" 'As for me I'd like to have money.' "

" 'The most difficult performance is acting naturally, isn't it?' "

" 'As soon as I was outside the door the wind, an old enemy, sprang at me.' "

" 'I shouldn't know you again if we did meet, you are so exactly like other people.' "

" 'Good morning, Mother. How did you rest?' "

Eventually they exhausted themselves. So much had been said and said so many times. Although weary of the game, Ina was far from weary of Babette's elocution. Even at a higher pitch and volume, Babette's voice retained its harmonies and carried its own echo.

Afterward they sat in silence, appreciating the quiet. And then again there was noise. Someone on the lawn was trying to reach the note of a song beyond her vocal range. Someone in the hallway was pushing a mop.

Babette yawned and moved to her bed, leaving one leg to dangle over the edge. For a while Babette's leg swung like a pendulum. Then Babette's leg wound down.

Ina stretched to pick up the sheet of paper Babette had left on the floor. It had been smudged by Babette's fingerprints but contained no other markings because Babette had an excellent memory. When they were living with Aunt Careen, Babette had once memorized an entire cookbook, including the page numbers of each recipe. Ina supposed Babette would have memorized something else if something else had sat on Aunt Careen's shelf. She supposed the example of Babette memorizing a cookbook was an example of what people called "making do."

SIX

AT SOME HOUR of the night ducks flew in and laid claim to the pond. Babette and Ina were among the first on the scene. From pond level, the walls behind the pond were barely noticeable, disguised by cascading ivy.

The ducks did not seem to mind the walls or an audience but there was discord among them. They swam in tight circles, bickering. Suddenly one flapped its way onto solid ground. The other ducks watched, still paddling. It was almost as if they had sent an envoy to test conditions, an expendable scout. The envoy-scout continued to pad about but kept its distance from the humans.

Unaccountably someone named Phoebe ran at the envoy-scout duck with a branch and began to thrash at its head. A chorus of human moans went up and up into the trees. The ducks in the pond flew and landed, flew and landed in great confusion. Ina had been too stunned to move but Babette vaulted toward Phoebe's branch and liberated it. Phoebe did not fight to keep the branch but would have lost the branch pull, regardless. Angry, Babette could be very tenacious. When they returned to Babette's room, Babette's eyes were still as dark as the pond. For dinner that night the kitchen served chicken.

SEVEN

THE EXCITEMENT of the day lingered. Even the dust motes seemed unusually agitated. Someone whose room was closer to the stairway had been banging her dinner tray like a drum but then another someone had taken the tray away. Ina stretched out on her mattress and held a hand over her eyes to block out the skittering shadows created by the outside floodlights.

At Aunt Careen's she had slept in a converted pantry. Aunt Careen had apologized profusely for the inadequate accommodations, but in fact Ina had loved where she slept at Aunt Careen's. There were multitudes of shapes to study on the paneled walls and layers of oddities in the wormwood. She suspected, although she shared the suspicion with neither Aunt Careen nor Babette, that a thorough survey of the pantry walls would take longer than her childhood.

The single pantry window had four blocks of panes, each of which had reacted differently to outside pressures. One had come loose from the wood and rattled in the slightest breeze. Another was a bird poop magnet. Before getting into bed, Ina covered the pantry window with a flowered tablecloth that Aunt Careen no longer considered dining room quality.

The window in her room here was taller than she was and could not be covered even if Ina somehow scrounged enough material to do so. It was a rule. No covered windows. Ina, like every resident, had to leave her room during the inside window-washing sessions but was allowed to watch the outside window washers go about their business, turning and twisting their implements to get between the bars. Now and again one of the workers would knock a pail off the platform or drop the squeegee. Should it start to sprinkle, the outside window washers labored on, hoping, Ina supposed, that the sprinkle belonged to a sun shower rather than presaged a coming deluge. As of yet, none of the outside window washers had stopped their washing to stare between the bars and through the window at her. Should that happen, Ina planned to wave in a nonchalant, calm and friendly fashion and perhaps to mouth "hello."

It was going to be a bad night for Ina. She could tell by how long she had already been covering her eyes. Her ears refused to stop listening although they were not listening for anything specific. The sheet stuck to her legs. The skin behind her knees prickled. Tomorrow Babette would look at her with concern because Ina would look the truth, that she had not slept at all well. In Ina's first week here, Isabelle of the long black ponytail had told Ina she would be a fool not to accept the night medications offered, but Babette had cautioned against it.

"Who knows what you might need to be capable of one midnight?" Babette asked to support her stance.

Babette had never had trouble sleeping anywhere she spent the night.

Once near bedtime at Aunt Careen's, Ina had lured Babette into the pantry bedroom to view a wormwood swirl of some beauty.

It had been a tight squeeze. Babette had to shimmy between the wall and the bed.

"The swirl has been there all along, of course," Ina said. "But I only found it last night."

"When last night?" Babette asked.

Babette's question did not sound altogether like an unencumbered question. It sounded like a question that already towed an answer.

"Can't remember," Ina said.

"Was it late?"

"Pretty late."

"Later than this?"

"Maybe a little," Ina said.

As was wildly apparent, Babette did not share Ina's fascination with wormwood swirls.

"Ina," Babette said. "Sleep isn't out to get you."

"I know," Ina said, knowing no such thing. Not even Babette could convince her that sleep had no dog in the fight.

Shimmying her way out, Babette burped a laugh.

"What?"

Ina had already settled beneath the covers.

Babette lifted the edge of Aunt Careen's crocheted quilt.

"This," Babette said, still smiling.

The quilt was red. And yellow. And pink. And orange. The edges were mostly mustardy green, though the edge nearest Ina's neck looked more the color of moss than mustard. The design of Aunt Careen's madcap creation did not look especially pre-considered but the overall effect was very, very bright.

"Aunt Careen's quilts and us," Babette said. "A funny bunch."

Laughing with Babette had been just the ticket. Ina had fallen fast asleep that night and stayed asleep until Aunt Careen called her to a breakfast of cinnamon toast. If she had dreamed, her dreams had not been populated by reptiles or parakeet deaths. No faces had become other faces. Dream Ina had not suddenly found herself on the edge of a very high and crumbly cliff.

She woke lying on her side, a pins and needles arm crooked under her head. Someone on the floor above was howling. The voice didn't sound like Clara's but might have been. Even after Ina sucked in and the wind of her breath offered no competition, Ina could not positively identify the distressed. She only knew the howl was not Babette's.

EIGHT

CLARA HAD SLIPPED the drawing under Ina's door when Ina and Babette were at the pond. To find a drawing on the floor was unexpected. Entering, both Ina and Babette had to leap to the sides to avoid stepping on it.

For a while they examined the drawing where it lay.

"A tree in the city. That's nice," Ina ventured.

"Only the one, though," Babette said.

"Why do you think Clara chose my door?"

"Probably an apology," Babette said. "For last night."

"Because she woke me?"

"Probably."

Ina gingerly picked up the drawing. It did not look as if it would stand up to too much handling.

"I'll have to find and thank her," Ina said.

That would be a task that would require not only effort but skill. Although Ina had not known Clara for very long, she knew that Clara liked to hide.

"When you do find Clara, tell her we both like her noisy drawing," Babette said.

After peering at the drawing a bit more, Babette extended her compliments to include the busy skyline.

Then Babette drifted elsewhere, humming.

Ina suddenly felt very peevish with Babette. Babette could wander off and ignore the drawing because Clara had not slipped the drawing under Babette's door.

The problem with gifts, Ina fretted, was the responsibility. Gifts required caretaking. They required enduring attention. When Aunt Careen had given Ina a delicate antique wristwatch for her fifteenth birthday, Ina had of course felt grateful and touched but also distraught. It was a beautiful watch with a gold band and tiny gold hands that had been kept in the safe sanctuary of Aunt Careen's jewelry box for untold years. Now it would become imperiled on Ina's wrist. It was not a sturdy watch, and Ina had not been a terribly coordinated teenager. Those two truths alone were enough to give pause. Ina could not bear to think of losing the watch or damaging it because of some fumbling clumsiness on her part that would, in turn, break Aunt Careen's heart.

"You won't break Aunt Careen's heart whatever happens to the watch," Babette had said at the time.

Babette assumed people who had shown unusual strength and fortitude on one occasion would continue to do so, no matter what.

Babette was not a doubter.

Clara's drawing was too fragile to pin to the wall, even if pinning were allowed. One of the edges had already gotten torn, either by Ina or Clara. The paper was too floppy to prop against the baseboard. If left near the window, Clara's small drawing might get sucked out by a strong draft and flown elsewhere. All sorts of horror scenarios bloomed in Ina's mind. What if the drawing sailed all the way to the pond, dropped and sank? What if the ducks mistook it for a strange new edible and before realizing it was not at all tasty mangled the bottom half? What if for fun or meanness Isabelle snatched it off an air current and proceeded to rip it to shreds? What if someone other than Isabelle saw Clara's drawing exit Ina's window and reported it as a projectile note that had been intended to crest the wall?

Babette was still humming.

Ina decided to return the drawing to Clara and act as if all along Clara had expected its return.

Babette thought that strategy might work.

"But when you hand it to Clara, make sure Clara believes what you're saying. If she starts to chew her tongue, tell her I wanted to keep it in my room but you were sure

EIGHT

Clara would want her lovely drawing back, so you brought it to her instead of me."

Ina found Clara sitting very quietly on the stairs. Clara looked from the drawing in Ina's hand to Ina's face.

Twice Ina cleared her throat. Babette would have handled the exchange with much more finesse.

"Your wonderful drawing," Ina managed to get out before losing the wherewithal to continue.

No one bothered them on the stairs, despite Ina's high hopes for interruption.

Ina waited for inspiration to strike.

Clara waited along with her.

NINE

SLIPPING HER FEET into her inside slippers, Ina noticed that her ankles looked smaller, slimmer. Her socks, collapsed onto themselves, resembled ruffles. The thumb and middle finger of her right hand easily encircled her left wrist. Ina did not believe that used to be the case.

Until the afternoon when she had come to visit Babette and had not left, given a choice, Ina chose chocolate over any kind of green food, whether for breakfast, lunch, dinner, midmorning or late-night snack. Aunt Careen had also been a fan of chocolate, favoring the bittersweet variety. Since Ina liked all chocolate equally, she was more than content to sit by the fire with Aunt Careen and share a plate of bittersweet. Given her chocolate enthusiasm, when previously visiting Babette, Ina would have brought along a box of assorted chocolates—assorted, because the preferences of Babette's sweet tooth varied according to Babette's mood. But chocolate was not allowed.

Ina did not think a lack of chocolate alone could account for her shrinking ankles. True, she had not consumed a chocolate bar, nugget, bonbon, slice of cake, ice cream cone or truffle for a while now, but neither had Babette, and Babette had not diminished. Babette had thickened. Lying on her bed, Babette's belly no longer sank beneath her ribs.

When Ina showed Babette her puddled socks, Babette was not overly concerned.

"Request smaller socks," Babette said.

Babette had missed Ina's point. It was very unlike Babette to hit so wide the mark.

Ina pulled at her socks.

"You can't not eat," Babette said, getting warmer.

"Do you remember the Easter Aunt Careen baked macaroons?" Ina asked.

"Burned the macaroons, you mean," Babette said.

Aunt Careen had not been wrong in her assessment that the macaroons belonged in the trash. But Ina and Babette had sprung into action to prevent that transfer from happening, convinced a pile of discarded burnt macaroons would have made their aunt's night a misery. After scraping off the most overtly crispy curlicues of coconut, Ina and Babette popped what was left into their mouths. They had been more inspired than careful in their scraping, so some of what they chewed tasted like ash. Regardless, they kept up the yummy noises for Aunt Careen's sake. Conferring afterwards, Ina and Babette had congratulated themselves on their quick wits and ability to carry the charade to its brilliant conclusion. As it turned out, they had not been successful after all. Aunt Careen remained terribly upset by the baking failure. It preyed on their aunt's mind until the Fourth of July and the inaugural gingerbread cookoff when Aunt Careen's pinwheel flags captured the heart of every patriotic judge.

"I miss . . ." Ina admitted.

"Of course," Babette said.

Although she was shrinking and Babette expanding, Ina felt calmer than when she had first noticed her diminishment because Babette again knew what she was thinking and required no further explanation. This return to normal was especially fortunate because explanations had begun to give Ina trouble. Lately being asked what she meant or why she had said what she had said or why she had said what she had said but no more and no less left Ina quite tongue-tied. Landing an explanation had become as iffy as flattening a mosquito. Both adversaries could be sneaky. Both could arrive and depart in a flash. And there was no question that Ina had lost a good bit of her former speed. Becoming a slowpoke had put her at a disadvantage all around.

TEN

MOSQUITOES had lately been much on Ina's mind. As well as she could remember before she came to visit Babette and never left, a mosquito sounded very loud at night when the lights were out and medium loud in daytime. Although Ina had now become less than swear-on-her-life certain that nighttime mosquito attacks trumped daytime mosquito attacks in terms of noise, part of her stubbornly held to her earlier belief.

With justification, she felt.

If Ina could not successfully rebut the countertheory that mosquitoes came at her at the same decibel day and night, she would have to accept that she was the variable, that there was a nighttime Ina reacting and a daytime Ina reacting. More alarming, that the nighttime/daytime Ina reacting to mosquitos *here* was not the same nighttime/daytime Ina who had reacted to bloodsuckers elsewhere.

The shift was not a personality update Ina cared to endorse.

According to Babette, anyone who arrived here and failed to depart was presumed to possess an extreme sensitivity to noise.

"So no loud sneezing during quiet hours," Babette said, "or you'll be lashed to the mast."

Ina must have looked petrified because Babette retracted the warning at once.

"I kid," Babette said. "Sometimes I forget you're still a rookie."

Ina was not swear-on-her-life certain she *was* still a rookie.

It seemed to her that quiet hours could fast make a veteran of anyone.

ELEVEN

BABETTE AND INA sat on their favorite bench with their favorite view of the pond, each under a black umbrella. It was not raining but it was so very, very hot and they had no hats.

They had to keep the umbrellas entirely upright. Otherwise the umbrellas tangled and pitched and exposed one or another of their arms to the sun.

Aunt Careen never got farther than the porch without a hat on her head. She had suggested Babette and Ina follow her example but did not insist. Too much sun emphasized Babette's freckles, particularly the cluster on her nose. Ina had envied Babette's freckles for no other reason than that the freckles were part of Babette. Silly, really. In many ways, Ina supposed, she had been a very silly child. Yet no one had previously called her scatterbrained. She had never been accused then as now of losing the thread.

The heat had turned the ducks in the pond torpid. They still paddled about but with little enthusiasm and kept mostly within the shade of the bulrushes. Not a whiff of breeze stirred the tops of the trees or Babette's or Ina's umbrella.

The bench was barely long enough to seat Ina and Babette comfortably. Nonetheless, Isabelle refused to be dissuaded and weaseled in, pushing and shoving to clear herself a space.

It was so much hotter, scooched up against Isabelle's salty self. The only advantage Ina could glean from the current seating arrangement concerned mosquitoes. Anyone would have better luck swatting a sweat-stuck mosquito.

Regarding the problem of Isabelle, Ina relied on Babette. Isabelle's manic rocking rocked all three of them and showed no sign of stopping. The combination of heat, stickiness and rocking sorely tested Ina's temper. Babette had lifted the hair off her neck but her face remained composed, noncommittal, probably because Babette was not the person hemmed-in between. One whole side of Babette's body was free to do as it pleased.

"Last night both entrance doors flew open, front and back," Isabelle said.

"When?" Babette asked, suddenly as alert as a cat.

"Midnight," Isabelle said. "Wide open. Wide enough for a truck. Or a bus. Or a zoo full of animals to pass through."

Ina frowned. A sliding bead of sweat briefly blurred her vision but there was no question she had heard what she had heard. The entrance doors were oversized, yes, but hardly wide enough to accommodate the kind of traffic Isabelle described. Maybe a golf cart could get out and in without scraping the doorframes. Maybe.

"Exactly at midnight?" Babette asked.

"Exactly," Isabelle said.

Isabelle's black braid had collected twigs of some sort. She looked as if she were sprouting. It was far from winter but her lips were badly chapped due to her tongue constantly tracing the outline of her mouth.

When Isabelle shrieked "Ha!" both Ina and Babette startled. They were better prepared for the second "Ha!" though not for the emphatic stomp.

"No idea I saw them!" Isabelle bragged, immensely impressed with herself.

Ina wished for many things simultaneously: a less hot day, someone else to hold her umbrella and more distance from Isabelle and Isabelle's eruptions. She did not get any of her wishes.

Astoundingly, Babette remained intrigued.

"How did you keep them from seeing you?" Babette asked, as if she were consulting with someone wholly reasonable.

"Because of where I was, of course," Isabelle said with utter disdain.

"And where was that?" Babette asked.

"The rafters!" Isabelle bellowed. "Where else?"

Ina could think of multiple where elses but would not be drawn into a tit for tat with Isabelle. She would endure being pasted onto Isabelle's arm but she would not do tit for tat.

Ina's and Babette's silence further infuriated Isabelle. She almost choked on indignation.

"The rafters *where I sleep!*"

Ina could believe that Isabelle had slept long and hard *somewhere*. Huge lumps of sleep crud crusted the corners of Isabelle's eyes. But the ludicrous rafters claim caused Ina to lose every last spore of patience.

In losing patience, Ina was not alone. Isabelle stood, snarled and stomped off. Having become splinter wary, instead of sliding, Ina got up and sat down again near the end of the bench.

Babette had pursed her lips, deep in thought.

"No! Babette!"

Babette obviously did not believe Isabelle's estimate of the size of the cargo that could pass through the entrance doors but seemed less willing to dismiss the possibility that the front and back doors were unlocked for a certain period each night.

"Next you'll be saying you believe Isabelle actually does sleep in the rafters," Ina complained.

As a rule, Babette did not inhabit the category of Gullible Gull.

Ruminating, Babette forgot to hold her umbrella upright.

"Babette!"

Impervious to Ina's protest, Babette clicked her tongue.

"Definitely information worth knowing," Babette said.

Persecuted by heat, Ina prepared to faint.

TWELVE

THEY WERE REQUIRED to come back to the communal dining room after it was food free. Instead of rows of tables, rows of chairs had been set up. Babette had seen in-house plays performed previously but this was Ina's first in-house theatre experience. She was not optimistic.

"You will have to clap, regardless," Babette said.

Clara, on the first row, had already clapped twice.

Ina did not need to be told she had to clap. She had clapped for Clara's story. And even before she came to visit Babette and stayed there were times when she had had to clap because clapping was expected and not clapping would have boomeranged scrutiny her way. No one came out well in a boomerang scrutiny situation.

The stage consisted of the very clean floor between the first row of chairs and the wall. The dining room now smelled of air freshener instead of stewed corn. The folding chairs were brutal to sit in. Ina sincerely hoped it was a one-act play.

The two authors had to set up their own scenery and props. They leaned a large piece of plywood against the wall and draped it with a sheet.

"We wanted to draw the outlines of two pillows near the top but we weren't allowed to use a magic marker on the sheet," one of the actresses said.

The other actress said: "So just imagine our heads are on pillows."

"Yes, we have to stay," Babette whispered.

"I *know* that!" Ina hissed.

When Babette read her thoughts, she should read *all* of them.

"We also aren't allowed to turn down the lights. So just imagine it's a lot darker and we're in bed trying to go to sleep."

Ina glanced about. She would not put it past Isabelle to storm the stage and announce, as for herself, she slept fine in the rafters. But Ina did not anywhere see Isabelle's swishing black braid.

"I'll be playing the part of Fin."

"And I'll be playing the part of Wing."

Fin wore blue pajamas and had pulled her hair into a top knot ponytail. Wing wore yellow pajamas and had divided her hair into two side ponytails. Ina appreciated the help in distinguishing between the two of them. They looked very much alike. Even their eyebrows looked identical. Ina had never seen one without the other. She supposed others could say the same about her and Babette.

Fin and Wing leaned against the sheeted plywood, eyes closed. Then Fin jerked and opened her eyes. Wing opened her eyes but did not jerk. The silent sequence was supposed to establish that Fin was jumpier than Wing, Ina supposed. Being less jumpy would likely give Wing less to do.

WING: Nightmare?

FIN: No.

WING: Vision?

FIN: No.

WING: Pebble?

The Fin character reached behind and fingered her spine. "Maybe," she said about the pebble. Then she asked: "Is it . . .?"

When the Fin actress intended to express wonder, she opened her eyes very wide.

WING: Barely midnight, if that.

FIN: That's not good.

WING: It never is.

Ina was beginning to warm to the Wing character. She looked lost but wise.

FIN: I did fall asleep, though. For a little bit.

WING: Did you?

FIN: I actually think I did.

WING: Hmm.

FIN: I know what you're thinking.

WING: Do you?

Ina elbowed Babette. The elbowing jostled Babette but did not affect her posture.

In tandem Fin and Wing twisted on the plywood to face a piece of round paper taped to a chair. It was supposed to represent the moon. But the next round of dialog had nothing to do with moon. Ina regretted the oversight. She would have enjoyed a moon discussion. Too bright, too hidden, too distant, too spooky. Ego moon. Diva moon. Look at ME! ME! ME! moon. Everyone had an opinion about the moon on a nightly basis.

Fin pointed in the direction of the paper moon but not precisely at it.

FIN: Satellite!

WING: Airplane.

FIN: People sleep on airplanes.

WING: Sometimes.

FIN: Except, chances are, at least one—

TWELVE

WING: Is wide awake. Mind racing. Snap, crackle, pop.

Ina hoped this part of the play would not dwell on the widespread snap, crackle, pop affliction. To dwell on it was not entertaining.

Fin broke into song. Something about green meadows.

WING: Leave off.
FIN: You could have joined in.
WING: No thanks.
FIN: Maybe a different tune?
WING: Singing leads to thinking and thinking leads to...
FIN: Right.

For a count of ten Fin and Wing turned and twisted on plywood. The turning and twisting was convincing, but Fin's grimacing had too much of a theatrical air about it.

FIN: Quick! Most astonishing word?
WING: *Re-gur-gi-tate.*
FIN: Most terrifying?
WING: *Attempt.*

Wowed by that profundity, Ina spread her hands. Babette blocked the clap.

"Not yet," Babette said.

"Growing up," Fin said and Wing bolted up, which meant Wing bent double at the waist. Clara could probably see the character Wing's hair part, but Ina and Babette sat too far back.

WING: Go there and we'll *never* sleep!

Ina grabbed Babette's hand. She did not think she would be able to sit in a hard chair and listen to talk about hard childhoods.

FIN: Manhole.

WING: Rabbit hole.

FIN: Slippery slope.

WING: Slippery soap.

Fin and Wing commenced to hula dance from the waist up. All three ponytails bobbed.

FIN: Soap Bubble. Burst bubble. Bubblegum. Bubblehead.

WING: Beachhead. Blockhead. Thunderhead.

FIN: Thundercloud. Dust cloud. Cloudberry.

WING: Strawberry. Blackberry. Gooseberry.

FIN: Beriberi—

The hula-ing stopped. Wing rubbed her eyes.

WING: What if we just pretend?

FIN: Okay.

WING: Shoulders relaxed! Eyes closed!

FIN: Are your eyes closed?

Wing's eyes were sometimes closed but just as often her eyelids fluttered apart.

WING: Yesssss.

FIN: Are you . . . pretending?

WING: Yessssssss. Are you?

FIN: Yesssssssss.

They were not bad at pretending, Ina thought. Neither of them.

FIN: Remember in that film—

WING: You're wrong.

FIN: Am not.

WING: Are.

FIN: Am *not*. In that film when the *moon* collides with the earth—

Ina felt gratifyingly vindicated. Every script circled back to the moon.

WING: It's not the moon.

FIN: Is.

WING: Isn't.

FIN: The whole thing filmed in shadow, start to finish.

WING: Dark, darker, darkest.

FIN: Planet losing oxygen by the hour.

WING: Everyone breathless, dragging their feet.

FIN: So they set loose the horses. And huddle in a tent.

WING: Waiting for the crash.

FIN: The bam, the boom.

WING: The end.

"The end," Fin and Wing together repeated and bowed from the waist, still propped against plywood. The applause took a while to build because the play had put a certain percentage of the audience to sleep, which might have been its purpose, otherwise why would it have been allowed?

"Quite clever," Babette said as she and Ina took their leave.

Ina was not sure she would go quite that far in praise.

"There were some interesting parts," Ina said. "But the middle was a bit slow."

"Only if you thought you were watching two people instead of one."

It was a bold interpretation. Two voices in the same head arguing.

"Goodnight," Babette said, hugging Ina at Ina's door.

"Goodnight, Babette," Ina said.

And she did hope that the rest of the night for each of them would be unremarkably-dull-to-the-point-of-oblivion good. No beams from a ME! ME! ME! diva moon invading their rooms. No one voice in their heads getting the better of any other. A truce called among the rooms' objects. Their beds, just because they were beds, not assuming they held supremacy and deserved slavish devotion.

Ina had not tried singing herself to sleep since she lived at Aunt Careen's. Unfortunately she was unfamiliar with the song about green meadows. She would have to come up with another tune.

THIRTEEN

COME THE MORNING Ina could not locate Babette.

Ina checked all the usual places. Babette's room. The halls. The pond. The bench. The library. The communal dining room. Clean as the dining room appeared overall, a left behind scrap of moon had lodged beneath a counter.

Searching for Babette, Ina had to be careful not to imitate the speed of her racing heart.

Clara had not seen Babette.

Isabelle would not say whether or not she had seen Babette but the glint in Isabelle's eyes told Ina that Isabelle was too much enjoying Ina's upset. Ina considered slapping Isabelle purely as a matter of principle and might have done so had glinty-eyed Isabelle not pranced herself elsewhere.

Left to her own devices, Ina could not quell the panic. She dashed and darted in useless circles, closer and closer to the thicket of trees. The moral of every book that contained a forest, woods or merely a dozen trees was never ambiguous: stay out if you value your life, sanity and belief in the benignity of nature. Woods had gobbled up many a clueless wanderer.

Not that Babette was by any measure clueless.

Ina had not meant to put that idea out into the universe as fodder for universal sport. Wherever Babette was, Babette was on a well-planned, well thought-out adventure.

Although Ina did not find Babette in the woods or elsewhere, she herself was apprehended, very likely because of the darting and dashing. Asked what she was doing among the trees, Ina had the sense to say "mushroom hunting" rather than searching for the missing Babette. It was not her finest hour in the art and craft of prevarication. Mushroom hunting was not on the list of approved solo or group activities.

After again checking the halls and library, Ina returned to Babette's room. The bed was impeccably made, but then it would have been. Babette's sweater and raincoat were still in the closet. Not on hangers because hangers were not allowed but folded neatly on the shelf. Babette had many times demonstrated to Ina how to tuck the corners of folded clothes and folded sheets. If Ina had actually mastered the sequence, she would now be able to refold the sweater and raincoat of Babette's that she had disturbed.

From one second to the next Ina's throat constricted. She was very near to weeping. It was never advisable to openly weep. Anyone passing by might be able to hear the snuffling. Ina bit down hard on her lip and as an extra precaution stuffed a towel against the door sill. She could not reach the transom.

From the floor she looked at the ceiling.

In her pantry bedroom at Aunt Careen's the ceiling was pocked with dirt dauber nests. Stingers did not frighten Ina and their busy industry provided a show whenever Ina cared to watch. The ceiling of Babette's room offered no distraction whatsoever. There was not a dirt dauber or cobweb or spider to behold.

Ina had put it off and put if off but now looked window-ward. She would just have to get over herself and stand by the glass and bars to see what could be seen. Babette might be trying to signal to her from the lawn and Ina's avoidance of windows was preventing the communication.

When Babette came back, and of course Babette would come back, of course she would, Ina would have to stop herself from flinging her entire body at Babette's chest and holding on for dear life as Ina had done when Aunt Careen minus her gall bladder returned from the hospital. While Aunt Careen was away, she and Babette had agreed to tell no one they were living in a grown-up-free zone because Babette was quite sure someone with good intentions or too much time on her hands would show up at the door and begin an interrogation that neither Babette nor Ina cared to countenance. They had happily eaten three meals of peanut butter daily, pleasantly full after each round. Babette insisted they double down on their tooth brushing, which was prudent given the adhesiveness of peanut butter. Babette had loaded the washer with their underwear and pajamas three days after Aunt Careen departed and they took turns scrubbing every dish they used. They may have been orphans but they were well-disciplined orphans. To keep off the radar of nosy neighbors, they let no routine slide. They even polished their shoes, which they knew would also please Aunt Careen. No one came home from the hospital and wanted to see dirty shoes or a sink full of dishes.

Behind the pond, in front of the wall, Babette appeared almost as if Ina had blinked her into existence.

"Babette!" Ina called, not really expecting Babette to hear her above the grind of the lawnmowers but feeling much better having called out Babette's name.

Facing the wall, Babette was reaching over her head, the fingertips of her right hand swallowed by brick. Babette had a spectacularly long reach. When Babette was in high school, the girls' basketball coach had been constantly after her to join the team.

By the time Ina reached Babette, Babette had both hands on her hips.

"You see it, don't you?" Babette asked.

Ina saw nothing of overpowering interest. Merely to keep Babette company, Ina had been idly counting bricks. She had not quite counted to one hundred, which had vaguely been her goal.

"The handhole," Babette said.

Babette gestured to a chunk of missing brick much higher than Ina's head but not so much higher than Babette's.

"Wouldn't you know it," Babette said. "It's been there all along."

The former Fin and Wing had marked off a rectangle of soft ground near the pond with their heels and were rehearsing a new dramatic offering. Wrestling seemed to be involved. Both had slicked back their hair and pinned it tightly. Gone were the frivolous ponytails. Lunging at the former Wing, the former Fin impressively growled.

Ina waved as she and Babette passed but neither the former Fin nor the former Wing broke character to wave back.

"Don't take it personally," Babette said.

As relieved as Ina had been to reunite with the missing Babette and to be walking now beside her, the remark ruffled Ina's feathers. How was anyone to take anything

THIRTEEN

other than personally? Such a comment was beneath Babette. Babette did not usually trade in glib buck-up chatter.

Ina side-eyed Babette while keeping the pace.

As soon as Babette was less preoccupied, Ina intended to have a word with her cousin about glib buck-up chatter.

FOURTEEN

THE POND had been drained. Too much pond mud had transferred onto the polished floors.

It was a terrible development. The ducks were perplexed. The ducks were bewildered. The ducks could not believe their eyes. The ducks waddled into and back out of the once-pond on non-wet feet.

The vast majority of humans, including Ina, were forlorn. It had not been a vast pond and it had not been the prettiest pond. Scum and algae had had their way with it and even the water in its middle was far from clear. But it was a pond. The only pond.

Astonishingly, when Babette saw the waterless pond she broke into a grin.

"Babette! You loved the pond!"

"Yes," Babette said. "But how much more mud will end up on the polished floors because of a drained pond?"

Ina contemplated.

If they jumped into the pond and stomped the bottom sludge as if they were wine maids stomping grapes,

FOURTEEN

Babette had a point. But what if the punishment for that frolic was no lawn privileges forever? Ina did not think the chance to have some temporary mud fun outweighed the risk of having to gaze upon the lawn from windows.

"Another gaffe. Another goof," Babette said, still oddly elated.

Ina had no talent for enigmas or puzzles. She had been known to play a decent hand of gin rummy in her time but generally speaking she was not the sharpest tack in the box when it came to cracking codes or decrypting mysteries. Ina would just have to wait for Babette to reveal all.

Clara did not grin when she saw the drained pond. Her face collapsed on itself. She was inconsolable. For the entire afternoon Clara plucked leaves off nearby bushes and tossed them into the dry pond as incentive for the water to return and float them.

Without the pond, the view was wanting. There were, however, fewer mosquitoes.

"I intend to write a story about the pond," Clara told Babette and Ina on the entrance steps.

"Do," urged Babette.

Ina turned her face away and groaned as quietly as it was possible to groan. A story about a drained pond? And they would have to listen to it. Babette would insist they support Clara. Refusing to listen would be rude and almost certainly hurt Clara's feelings. Still, Ina did not like the idea of being a captive audience any time Clara decided to take up a stick of charcoal. Or pretended to.

"People are who they are, Ina."

No, Ina thought.

"Yes," Babette said.

Not always, Ina thought.

"More often than not," Babette said.

"There are people who want to change," Ina said.

Babette shrugged.

Aunt Careen, for instance, had once set her mind upon reducing and after denying herself cocoa, suet pudding, lemon squares, pancakes and butter, fried okra and fried ham, plus foregoing gravy on her morning biscuit, had lost twelve pounds and a dress size.

Babette tapped her skull.

"Inside, Ina. The same inside."

It was true that during all of Babette's time here, before and after Ina had also not been permitted to leave, Babette had not stopped being her essential self. Ina supposed that was a legitimate example of people being who they are and remaining that way. But the essential Babette also was a person who typically went against the grain, so there you were. Babette stood out in any context.

Ina left Babette's room and frownly returned to her own. Babette had never been able to read Ina's thoughts through a wall, not even the pantry's thin paneling at

Aunt Careen's, and Ina wanted to be alone with her thoughts for a spell.

It was hard to go against Babette and Babette's confidence. It always had been hard. But Babette's no-change theory was not the prevailing theory around these parts. For instance, since arriving and being unable to leave, Ina had been led to believe that her tendency to dart and dash as well as her fear of windows could be overcome.

Ina was all for losing a fear of windows. The world was plastered with windows. Overrun with windows. Maybe it was possible for someone to avoid a specific window but no one could squelch window awareness altogether. It could not be done. Ina had serially tried. Life would be infinitely less complicated if Ina transformed into a window rationalist. The dart and dash stuff she rather enjoyed, though. The dart and dash reflex she would rather retain.

FIFTEEN

THEY WERE TO BE TAKEN individually to the library and tested. Because of the necessary pencils involved they would be in the company of a watchful proctor.

Ina was scheduled to be tested before Babette, which was nervous-making in itself. It was an order neither liked. Babette because Babette worried what a nervous Ina might do when cornered with a test, and Ina because she had counted on Babette to remember all the questions and prep her in advance.

When the knock came, Ina and Babette were together. Ina had not been able to stomach the idea of breakfast so Babette had fasted along with her.

As the door swung on its hinges, grave as a nun Babette advised: "When in doubt, lie."

The proctor's squeaky-clean shoes squeaked on the hallway's polished floors. Ina hoped her own shoes carried no mud.

Mud on her shoes would have made for a bad start.

FIFTEEN

The library was scarcely recognizable. There was a new gray couch and the most tattered books on the four shelves had been culled. The dazzlingly white baseboards showed not a speck of grime. Entering, Ina did not have to suppress the urge to sneeze but she did grieve. She had liked the old library. When she pictured herself taking the test she had pictured being in the library as it had been, broken in like an old comfortable bathrobe. The dusty curtains had been removed but not replaced. If Ina lifted her head from the test page, naked windows would be in her face. Directed to the also new table, Ina averted her gaze from naked windows.

"Begin," the proctor said before Ina had found a comfortable position. Her hipbones were grinding into the also new cushionless chair.

Ina supposed she was expected to answer each and every one of the twenty questions on the page.

LEAST FAVORITE NUMBER:

Right off the bat Ina was stumped. She disliked "nine" but also disliked "one."

LEAST FAVORITE COLOR:

Ina glanced at the couch. "Gray."

WHILE VISITING BABETTE

LEAST FAVORITE WORD:

Wait a daggone minute, Ina thought. That question sounded awfully familiar. Was this a play? Was she in a play without knowing she was in a play? That would seem hardly fair.

The proctor's face offered no clues either way but her index finger twice tapped her wristwatch.

Reminding Ina that she was on the clock did nothing to hasten her responses, but the warning did send her into a memory warp that wasted several additional answering minutes.

They were in the gymnasium. Ina's class and the two classes above hers. It must have been spring because they took tests seated in desks moved into the gym every spring. Nonetheless, the memory preserved no specific spring-like details, not even so much as the chwirk of a hawk reverberating through the open gym doors. Perhaps she had been concentrating too hard on completing the test to register raptors. The desks had been placed far apart to prevent cheating. That Ina remembered. Also that the scoreboard clock was ticking off seconds and minutes. The scoreboard must have been the reason they took the tests in the gym, Ina now realized. No teacher had volunteered her wristwatch.

LEAST FAVORITE ANIMAL:

Snakes? Pigeons? Skunks? Hyenas? Reading the question twice did not help narrow the field. The spring school tests had been multiple choice.

LEAST FAVORITE FOOD:

"Mashed potatoes," Ina wrote, then erased. They had been served mashed potatoes only the night before. It seemed unwise to complain about last night's menu on a test. "When in doubt, lie," Babette had said. "Canned peaches," Ina wrote and underlined.

BOOK YOU NEVER FINISHED:

The true answer was *Moby Dick* but Ina somehow felt the preferred answer was the Bible. She wrote "The Bible," capitalizing the "t" in "the" to be on the safe side.

SONG YOU NEVER WANT TO HEAR AGAIN:

Easy peasy. "Young at Heart."

ITEM OF CLOTHING YOU WOULD NEVER WEAR:

Ina elected to treat shoes as clothing. "Flipflops," she wrote. She disliked the flapping.

FAVORITE OBSCENITY:

Surely a trick question. Ina swiftly read through the rest of the list.

SOMETHING YOU SAID BUT WISH YOU HADN'T:
WORST ADVICE YOU EVER GOT:
WORST ADVICE YOU EVER GAVE:
LAST WORDS BEFORE EXECUTION:

And more in that vein. Someone had decided to save the most incriminating questions for last.

Ina let her time expire without filling in any more answers. The proctor walked her back to her room where Babette was waiting.

For Babette, Babette seemed quite anxious.

"Well?"

"They've cleaned the library," Ina reported. "They took away the curtains and the green couch."

Babette looked crestfallen.

"Bastards," Babette said.

Babette would have no difficulty answering the favorite obscenity question.

SIXTEEN

THE TESTING was supposed to take care of the overcrowding, Isabelle told Ina and Babette. "Keep it under your hats," Isabelle said.

"Do you believe Isabelle?" Ina asked Babette once Isabelle and her snickering had departed.

"I don't disbelieve her," Babette said.

Yet it remained something of a wonder. The testing. The overcrowding. The suddenness of there being too few rooms, too few bedframes.

Ina and her mattress transferred over to Babette's room. As delightful as it was to overnight with Babette, Ina found making up a mattress on the floor difficult. In every instance the mattress slid about, defiant.

Throughout the day the hallway stayed busy with transport. Ina thought the dragged mattresses sounded like dragged bodies. Babette proposed a qualifier.

"If the body and mattress weigh the same."

"How much does a mattress weigh?" Ina asked.

"It took both of us to lift yours," Babette said.

"A substantial girl, then," Ina said.

"Very likely," said Babette.

"More substantial than me," Ina said.

"I would think," Babette said.

If Ina were being dragged down the hallway, Babette might not be aware, Ina thought.

"Yes, I would," Babette said.

When the hall noise faded, Babette stretched out on her bed to nap. Ina sat on her mattress and played Patience with a deck of cards missing the Queen of Diamonds. Aunt Careen called Patience "Ole Sol." Until Babette corrected her, Ina believed Aunt Careen was playing against an ancient man with a long white beard that only Aunt Careen could see. Ina had been glad to be shed of that notion.

Babette was not truly napping, Ina could tell.

"Babette?"

"Ina?"

"Babette?"

"Ina?"

"I want to talk about the day it happened," Ina said.

Babette raised up on her elbows. A hank of hair covered her left eyebrow.

"All right," Babette said.

"When I came to visit you, did I seem myself?"

"You did," Babette said.

"And we were having a normal Tuesday visit before it happened?"

"Perfectly normal," Babette said. "We discussed Aunt Careen's blue jar."

"And you told me I could hide under your bed. This bed."

Ina pointed.

"I did," said Babette. "After the incident got underway."

"Then why did I panic?" Ina asked.

"It was new for you," Babette said.

"Being locked in?"

"Yes," Babette said. "Being locked in."

Both fell silent. Ina worried the edge of the Queen of Hearts. She was not the first to have done so. The Queen of Hearts was looking quite mauled and shabby.

"The fault is mine, really," Babette said after further reflection.

Ina frowned in disagreement.

"It is," Babette insisted. "Because I should have described the sensation the first time you visited. Then you would have been less afraid."

Ina took a moment to sort her thoughts.

"Would I, though? Have been less afraid?"

Even if Ina had been armed with Babette's thorough description, the less-afraid outcome seemed a stretch.

Babette shrugged.

"You may be right. A description is not much of a preparation."

"You did tell me to hide," Ina said.

"Yes," Babette said. "I did do that."

"I should have listened," Ina said.

Again Babette's shoulders lifted and dropped.

"In retrospect I don't think hiding would have helped much."

That was what Ina thought, too. But she needed to hear Babette say it. Babette had been here longer. Babette knew better the outs and ins.

SEVENTEEN

IN THE MIDDLE OF THE NIGHT smoke curled into their room through the transom. Babette smelled it first. "Ina! Wake up!"

Ina had been dreaming of the Puritans. She must have thought the smoky scent came from their Thanksgiving feast.

Babette shoved Ina's feet into her outside slippers and pinched Ina's grogginess away.

"Wrap this around your face," Babette said.

Ina balked. It was Babette's best white blouse. The one with scalloped sleeves.

"Ina!"

In the hall they merged with a throng of outside-slippered feet being hurried toward the back entrance door. On the lawn there was a chorus of ragged coughing. Clara's teeth clacked. Everyone was shivering. They had all gone to sleep in their lightest nightgowns. Although smoke still wafted from the building, Ina saw no flames.

While Babette and Ina were living with Aunt Careen there had been a chimney fire in the house next door, a conflagration Aunt Careen's household had slept through until the fire trucks arrived. A misdirected fire hose shooting water at Aunt Careen's bedroom window woke her. Ina and Babette were made to stay inside while Aunt Careen joined her neighbors on the street carrying two of her crazy quilts, which Aunt Careen wrapped around her neighbors' shoulders. Babette and Ina took turns peeking out the front door at the spectacle. Ina had never seen so much red, yellow and orange at once, what with Aunt Careen's quilts and the fire truck and the fire fighters' suits and the fire itself. When the neighbors moved away, stray cats moved in, one of them orange.

"Remember the orange cat?" Ina asked Babette.

"Vicious," Babette said.

Babette's slur was apt. It had been a vicious cat. The moment it smelled human the claws came out.

The next morning all the residents were turned out onto the lawn again so that the cleaners could clean everything, top to bottom. Ina had grown rather fond of the smoke smell. She could almost imagine she and Babette were camping.

Clara found Babette and Ina near the drained pond but not in it. Although Clara had not run to reach them since running, even in the case of fire, was forbidden,

SEVENTEEN

Clara needed to catch her breath before confiding that last night's fire had started in the rafters.

Ina and Babette gaped in tandem.

"Are you sure, Clara?" Babette asked. "This isn't the start of a story?"

Between shallow breaths Clara shook her head.

Babette narrowed her eyes not at Clara but at the scorched building behind them.

"Do you know how the fire started?" Babette asked.

"Matches," Clara said.

Ina looked at Babette. Where had Isabelle gotten matches? Matches were as tightly guarded as keys.

"Say what you will, Isabelle is resourceful," Babette said.

Babette's tone had shifted from surprised to alarmingly admiring.

"Resourceful" was not the adjective Ina would have used. She hoped Babette would also think better of that accolade. Isabelle was barmy.

Clara either had not heard Babette or pretended not to hear or now actually was in the midst of making up a story about fire and matches.

Isabelle immortalized in a story.

Ina could just puke.

EIGHTEEN

THEY HAD BEEN TURNED OUT of the building for the second day straight. The cleaning was taking longer than expected. The reconstruction of the rafters had also left a sawdust mess.

Since Babette and Ina had walked briskly from the entrance steps to their favorite bench they had foiled the competition. For now.

Mercifully the sun umbrella season had passed. One could sit on the bench and feel neither pickled nor boiled. The trees that would lose leaves still had them, though tints other than green were gaining ground. Not too many mornings from now they were bound to wake up to frost.

Babette had been in residence for several frosts, of course. Sometimes it took until noon for the lawn to unthaw, Babette said. Babette thought waiting for frost to melt too tedious for words.

If pressed to choose between a solid frost and mushy grass, Ina would opt for frost.

EIGHTEEN

"And then as soon as there's frost, everybody catches cold," Babette continued, sounding immoderately exasperated.

On the rare, previous occasions when Babette had expressed exasperation, frost and head colds had not been the cause of her pique. Ina was fairly certain that the true source of Babette's exasperation today was also unrelated to frost and head colds. But where Babette decided to aim her exasperation was entirely up to Babette. There could be no arguing with that.

"We will have to bring out the scarves and sweaters. We will have to bundle up," Ina said as if this were startling news.

Babette did not take Ina's wardrobe bait. Because Babette's gaze seemed fixed on the wall beyond the pond, Ina fixed her gaze accordingly. The wall was totally cast in shadow. Frost would form there first.

Regrettably, Ina was highly susceptible to head colds. A teacher had told Aunt Careen Ina had weak lungs and suggested Ina sleep with a hot water bottle on her chest. Aunt Careen had complied, sending Ina off to the pantry at night with a new red companion. But the hot water bottle had made Ina sweat and sweating had made her sheets damp. Babette took umbrage. Sleeping on damp sheets would make anyone, strong-lunged or otherwise, ill, Babette said, after which Aunt Careen saw reason. Thereafter, by three-way agreement, the wayward teacher's name had been excised from the household's vocabulary. To make sure Aunt Careen did not falter in her resolve, Babette buried the red water bottle behind the nodding tea roses.

Ina was on the verge of reminding Babette about the buried hot water bottle when Clara appeared with the actresses.

"I have another story," Clara said, then squished between Babette and Ina on the bench and so placed drew her knees to her chin. Fortunately the perspiring season had passed.

The former Fin and Wing remained standing and warmed up their voices with trills.

"Is it a pond story?" Babette asked kindly.

"Is it about sisters?" Ina asked less kindly.

"Neither," Clara said.

Ina could not decide whether to feel glad or beleaguered in advance by a Clara-selected story that incorporated neither a drained pond nor sisters. No ponds and no sisters might leave Clara swinging blind.

Do *not* ask what it's about, Ina thought, trying to transfer that admonition into Babette's brain and failing.

"What's your new story about, Clara?" Babette asked.

"It's a crow story requiring three readers," Clara said.

"I will be reading the part of Arthur," the former Wing said.

"And I will be reading the part of Ezekiel," the former Fin said. "Ezekiel is head of the Crow Collective."

Ina supposed that meant that the former Fin had won the starring role.

"We will both simultaneously read the part of Tobias," the former Wing continued, "and Clara will read the stage directions."

So *not* a story, another play, Ina thought. And *not* reading, reciting, since none of the three held a sheaf of pages. She wished people would call a play a play and be done with it.

"Is there a title, Clara?" Babette asked.

"Two," Clara said, disclosing neither before announcing the setting. "Upper story of abandoned derelict building. Large, glass-less window with view of highway."

Ina squirmed. A play featuring windows.

CLARA: Arthur forlornly gazes toward the highway. Ezekiel enters.

EZEKIEL: I thought to find you here. The darker the day, the darker the mind.

ARTHUR: And now that I am found? What next, Ezekiel? Order me elsewhere? Insist I put behind me the sights and sounds of Tobias's hard end on macadam? You have always presumed to know what's best—for all of us.

Ina tried to catch Babette's eye. Although the former Wing and Fin were impressively rising to the challenge of exalted language, Clara should not be encouraged to go around claiming she wrote everything she read. She really should not.

> EZEKIEL: I presumed you wished to mourn alone. As you have. For many hours. Now come. Solitude is not for our kind.
>
> ARTHUR: Tobias is dead. I have no kind.
>
> EZEKIEL: Such thoughts do you no honor, Arthur. Nor Tobias. Fate is fate. It was his time.
>
> ARTHUR: Tobias was *twelve*! A crow's midlife.

Ina scanned the nearby lightning poles for crows. A real crow audience would have heightened the impact.

> EZEKIEL: Twelve years lucky. Why not take that view of the matter?
>
> ARTHUR: Can you not *understand*? We flew together. We *flew*.

The former Wing flapped her arms.

EZEKIEL: And you—with others—will fly again.

ARTHUR: No.

EZEKIEL: This sky-dread you suffer. It will pass.

ARTHUR: I do not dread *sky*.

EZEKIEL: Then return to it.

ARTHUR: As if Tobias had not died? Or *lived*? As if memory died with him?

EZEKIEL: As a crow who has learned a useful lesson.

ARTHUR: Tobias did not fall to a hunter's gun or predator's snare. He was not captured by a devil child for sorcery's sake. His death was random, senseless. A miscalculation of wind. An automobile's blunt steel. Go, Ezekiel. Your duty here is done. You have offered counsel and been refused. Leave me to my grief.

EZEKIEL: And what would you have me tell the flock?

ARTHUR: What I have told you. I will not fly again.

It occurred to Ina that she was not much of a melodrama fan. But perhaps any play about crows was destined to be filled with loud, histrionic speeches.

"A crow who does not fly is no crow," the former-Fin-now-Ezekiel warned.

ARTHUR: Then consider me crow no longer.

Babette squeezed Clara's left knee.

Ina could not fathom why Clara needed comforting over the behavior of a rebellious crow.

> **CLARA:** Ezekiel turns his back on Arthur, speaks only to the audience.
>
> **EZEKIEL:** And with this he goes too far. The posturing antics of a maudlin crow. I will not have our flock twice reduced, the second by means of sentiment.

Good call was Ina's first reaction. But then she realized everyone was supposed to be on Arthur's side. Even if Arthur was a pill.

Clara announced Ezekiel's exit but no one moved.

> **CLARA:** The moon rises, streaming light on Arthur. The ghost crow Tobias enters, dragging a wing.
>
> **ARTHUR:** Tobias . . . ? Is it . . . ? Could it be . . . ? Has grief contrived your image?
>
> **TOBIAS:** You see what you see, Arthur. It's me. Stuck here evermore. But why are you here, Arthur? You should have launched hours ago.

And Clara should have recruited an extra someone to play the role of Tobias. Arthur reciting Tobias's part would have been confusing. Ezekiel reciting Tobias's part would have been confusing. Both reciting Tobias's part at once was impossibly distracting. The only remedy, Ina decided, was to listen while staring at her lap.

TOBIAS: If you're hanging around because of what happened to me, don't. There's no undoing that. Plus, turns out: being dead's not so awful.

CLARA: Arthur's feelings are deeply hurt.

ARTHUR: You miss nothing? No one?

TOBIAS: I'd rather be flying, sure. But if I'm honest there's a lot of stuff I don't miss. Top of the heap: Ezekiel and his rules.

ARTHUR: And you are . . . completely on your own? Without a Collective?

CLARA: Discomfited by Arthur's questions, Tobias does not answer. Noises of approach.

TOBIAS: Enjoy the crow life, my friend. Range far and wide. Roam the skies for both of us.

ARTHUR: Tobias! Stay!

CLARA: Tobias waves his unbroken wing, exits.

To Ina, Clara said: "You can open your eyes now. The ghost crow is gone."

"My eyes weren't closed," Ina said in defense of her honor. She was not afraid of ghost crows or any other sort of ghost and knew well how rumors got started.

Babette raised a finger to her lips.

CLARA: Ezekiel enters.

EZEKIEL: Have you now come to your senses, Arthur?

WHILE VISITING BABETTE

CLARA: Arthur does not respond.

EZEKIEL: And what is your plan? To perpetually mourn and mope, dragging tail feathers across these splintery boards? Without the protection of the flock, you and your moroseness are easy prey. A tasty treat for feral cats and rabid raccoons, the enterprising badger.

ARTHUR: If I die as you predict, I die. Tonight has taught me to be less afraid of death.

EZEKIEL: And your flock? What of them? Is there no end to your selfishness?

ARTHUR: Mockery will not change my decision.

EZEKIEL: A decision not yours to make.

ARTHUR: I disagree.

CLARA: Ezekiel strong-arms Arthur to the window.

Except, to Ina's relief, there was no actual window on the lawn and even if Arthur and Ezekiel play-acted fisticuffs, the loser would at most tip over versus parachute.

EZEKIEL: In time you will thank me, Arthur. The solitary crow is a danger to himself and others. Once aloft you will again exult in the charms of flight, the exhilarating freedom of elevation.

CLARA: Arthur struggles against the restraints.

ARTHUR: *This* is *freedom*? You have repeated the lie so often you believe it true.

EZEKIEL: I have told our story. The crows' story. As I will continue to do. Proudly.

CLARA: Ezekiel shoves Arthur out the window.

But not really, Ina reminded herself.

CLARA: Ezekiel remains at the window, watching.

EZEKIEL: How he fights against flapping! As if his will is stronger than pedigree!

CLARA: Gradually Ezekiel's amusement fades, replaced by anger and contempt. It is unclear whether Arthur flapped his wings or willfully fell to earth.

When Clara cawed, Ina lurched sideways. Miraculously she did not pick up a splinter.

After Clara and her troupe had departed arm-in-arm, Ina said: "I'll guess first. One of the titles of the play not written by Clara is 'For Love of Crow.'"

"Nice," said Babette.

Ina appreciated the compliment. She did think "For Love of Crow" had a certain deterministic flair.

Babette opted for an action title. "Resistance."

NINETEEN

"Another something I should have mentioned earlier," Babette said.

With difficulty Ina surmounted the temptation to stuff her ears.

She did not want to hear about another something that should have been mentioned but was not. Babette had withheld whatever it was for a reason. Ina trusted Babette's initial instincts. The whatever should remain undisclosed.

"There was another lockdown shortly before you arrived."

Neither by word nor deed did Ina encourage Babette to proceed.

"Because of Clara," Babette said.

Ina could not outwait Babette. It was futile to try.

"Oh all right. Tell me. What about Clara?"

Clara, Ina knew, had been here even longer than Babette. Ina knew that Clara preferred to go barefoot. Ina knew that Clara liked to hide from time to time. Ina knew that Clara had no qualms about calling a play a story. That was the gist of what Ina knew about Clara.

"When Clara hurt herself, they locked everybody in," Babette said.

"What do you mean by 'hurt herself'?"

It was not like Babette to be so deliberately indeterminate. Babette had shown Ina the dying-then-dead robin that had smacked the porch post when Ina was eight because Babette said both she and Ina were in no position to be squeamish. They were orphans. But Clara was not dead. They both knew that.

"How did Clara hurt herself, Babette?"

"The wrist bandages actually looked like tennis cuffs," Babette said.

There were splotches on Babette's cheeks. One of Babette's hands picked at the other.

Ina felt awful. For forcing Babette to say more than Babette wanted to say and for not being as kind to Clara as Ina should have been.

Babette leaned her head on Ina's shoulder.

"Clara will need you."

When Ina's shoulder twitched, Babette's head bobbed.

"What do you mean?" Ina asked for the second time in too few minutes.

"Just look after her when she needs looking after."

Ina had never been good with responsibility. Never, ever. She lost barrettes. She lost socks. Aunt Careen had started the Ina Replacement Fund when Ina was ten, which was less cruel than the title suggested. Aunt Careen did not intend to swap Ina for a more dependable child. As recently as last year, before Ina had come to visit Babette and stayed, Ina had misplaced both her driver's license and tooth guard on the very same day. She could not look after Clara. Clara would be better off being looked after by a lawn-mowing groundskeeper.

"I'm asking you to do it," Babette said. "For me."

Ina frowned. Ordinarily she would have quizzed Babette as to why Ina should be looking out for Clara *for* Babette when Clara clearly felt closer to Babette than she would ever feel to Ina, but Ina had already asked and been told too much of what she would rather not have learned this hour.

"Ina?"

"Babette?"

"Ina?"

"Babette?"

"For *me*."

"I heard you," Ina said.

But she would make no promises. Not to or for Babette.

[An ending that falls short of absolute comfort]

TWENTY

It was nearly midnight but neither Ina nor Babette was asleep. Ina had adjusted to sleeping on a mattress on the unforgiving floor but the weather had turned hot again. Even Babette was restless. Twice already Babette had gone to the window and remarked on the heat lightning.

"Come see," Babette said. "It makes the sky look like milk."

Babette must have forgotten how much they both disliked heat lightning as children, waiting, waiting, waiting for thunder that never arrived. Babette must also have forgotten how much Ina disliked milk. When her second-grade teacher forced Ina to open and "at least sip" from a carton of milk, Ina retaliated by becoming instantly ill. Aunt Clara had been concerned that Ina had developed a dairy allergy. Together Babette and Aunt Clara had searched Ina for marauding hives. Babette had instructed Ina to lick her lips to double check for swelling. There had been no swelling but there had been a residue of milk on

Ina's lips that caused her to be instantly ill again. Nothing dire was afoot. Ina simply despised straight-up milk.

"Ina? It looks really pretty. Each flash outlines the trees."

"I'm fine here," Ina said though that was not exactly the case. The hot sheets had tangled around her ankles and when she kicked at them she made the tangling worse.

The next flash of heat lightning illuminated a weirdly bulky Babette.

When Babette's bulk plopped onto Ina's mattress, Ina imagined she felt seasick. But Ina also understood that a bouncing mattress was not why her stomach churned.

Sitting next to Babette, Ina realized Babette was wearing another layer under her nightgown. Ina also noted that Babette was not wearing either her inside or her outside slippers.

Supremely uneasy, Ina silently counted to ten, then to twenty.

Babette needed to tell her something, Babette said.

"Or you could wait," Ina said, the same way she and Babette had waited for thunder.

Babette had reached a decision.

Babette had decided they no longer needed to be here.

Babette had decided tonight was as good a time as any to leave.

TWENTY

Ina wondered whether Babette had discovered another way over the wall besides brick handholds. Aloud she said: "Have you?" because Babette had not responded to her thoughts.

"For the underlayer, wear what you were wearing the day you came to visit and stayed," Babette said.

The outfit Ina was wearing when she came here and did not leave could not be resurrected. She had been wearing a belt. She had not been allowed to keep the belt. Because she did not want to hear more of what Babette was saying, Ina occupied her mind with wondering what had become of her cloth belt, in whose closet or in which locker it hung.

"If we leave separately, we'll make less noise," Babette said. "I'll go first. We'll meet up at the pond."

So Isabelle had not lied. The entrance doors were open at midnight.

A horrid thought struck Ina.

"Is Isabelle coming too?"

"And give up her rafters?"

At least Ina had made Babette laugh.

Ina wanted to remember Babette laughing.

Holding Ina's trembling fingers made Babette's fingers tremble also.

"We can do this, Ina," Babette said. "You can do it. I'll be with you. We'll be doing this together."

Despite Babette's help and Babette's confidence, Ina did not think she *could* do it. On the lawn in heat lightning she might easily revert to dart and dash. And if Babette were still relying on brick handholds, Ina was not tall enough. If Babette tried to lift Ina up, Ina would get mud on Babette's traveling clothes. What if, even before she left the building, Ina saw Isabelle draped across the rafters and the fright made her squeal? What if in the dark hallway she lost her way on the way to the entrance doors? What if she suddenly remembered something she had left behind that she could not bear to be separated from and by running back to get it left Babette vulnerable by the pond, exposed by flashes of heat lighting?

There were also other impediments.

She had not yet learned to like mashed potatoes.

She had not yet learned to accept a story that was a play or a play that was a story.

She had taken tests but had neglected to answer all the questions.

Her file did not yet contain the term "progress."

Perhaps what they had said since she had come to visit Babette and stayed was truer than at first she believed: that she could not completely rely on what she thought or felt at any given time or place, that her brain had to be retrained.

TWENTY

Perhaps waffling over leaving or not leaving with Babette was just another example of what she had been told was "muddled thinking."

It was all so confusing.

"See you in a few," Babette said and kissed Ina's cheek.

The door squeaked.

When the door squeaked again, Ina's spirits lifted, hoping Babette had thought better of the getaway idea and returned. But the person stepping noiselessly in was not Babette.

"Have you been waiting all this time in the hall?"

Clara nodded.

"So I guess Babette never really thought I'd follow," Ina said.

"She thought there was a possibility you wouldn't," Clara said.

At the window Clara and Ina watched Babette, agile as a possum, scale the wall and disappear. She had left her nightgown behind. The heat lightning made Babette's nightgown look like an oversized magic mushroom.

Clara tapped the glass.

"I hate windows," Ina said.

Ina hated windows and now part of her wanted to stay forever at the window of the room that had been Babette's and then Babette's and Ina's, staring after her cousin, the escapee.

"Is it okay if I sleep in Babette's bed?" Clara asked.

"Tonight or every night?"

"Every," Clara said.

Ina's lips puckered. Her eyes spilled over. Babette had only just left and already Ina missed her terribly, totally.

No one could replace Babette.

"Of course not," Clara agreed.

A thought crept up on Ina.

If Clara actually wrote stories or plays she might next compose a story or play about Babette.

"Would you like that?" Clara timidly asked.

In her head Ina had to admit she might.

"Then I'll start at once," Clara said.

※

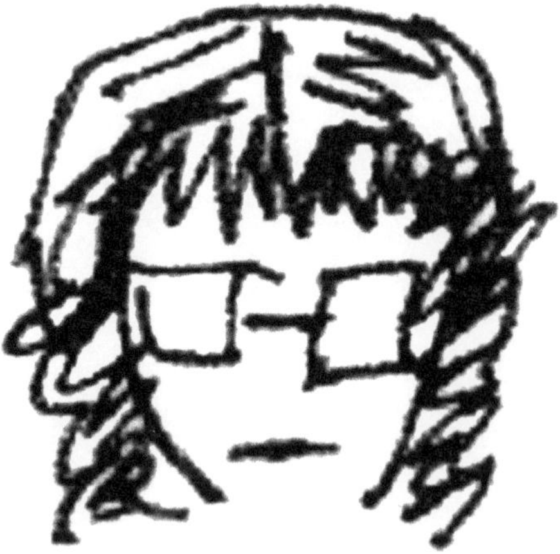

Kat Meads is the author of more than twenty books and chapbooks of poetry and prose, including the nonfiction collection *These Particular Women* (Sagging Meniscus, 2023). Her work has been recognized by fellowships from the National Endowment of the Arts, the Fine Arts Work Center in Provincetown, Yaddo and Montalvo Center for the Arts. She lives in California. (katmeads.com)

www.ingramcontent.com/pod-product-compliance
Ingram Content Group UK Ltd.
Pitfield, Milton Keynes, MK11 3LW, UK
UKHW040903120225
454898UK00015B/156